Daddy's Roommate

by Michael Willhoite

To my Dad

My Mommy and Daddy
got a divorce last year.

Now there's somebody new at Daddy's house.

Daddy and his roommate Frank live together,

Work together,

Eat together,

Sleep together,

Shave together,

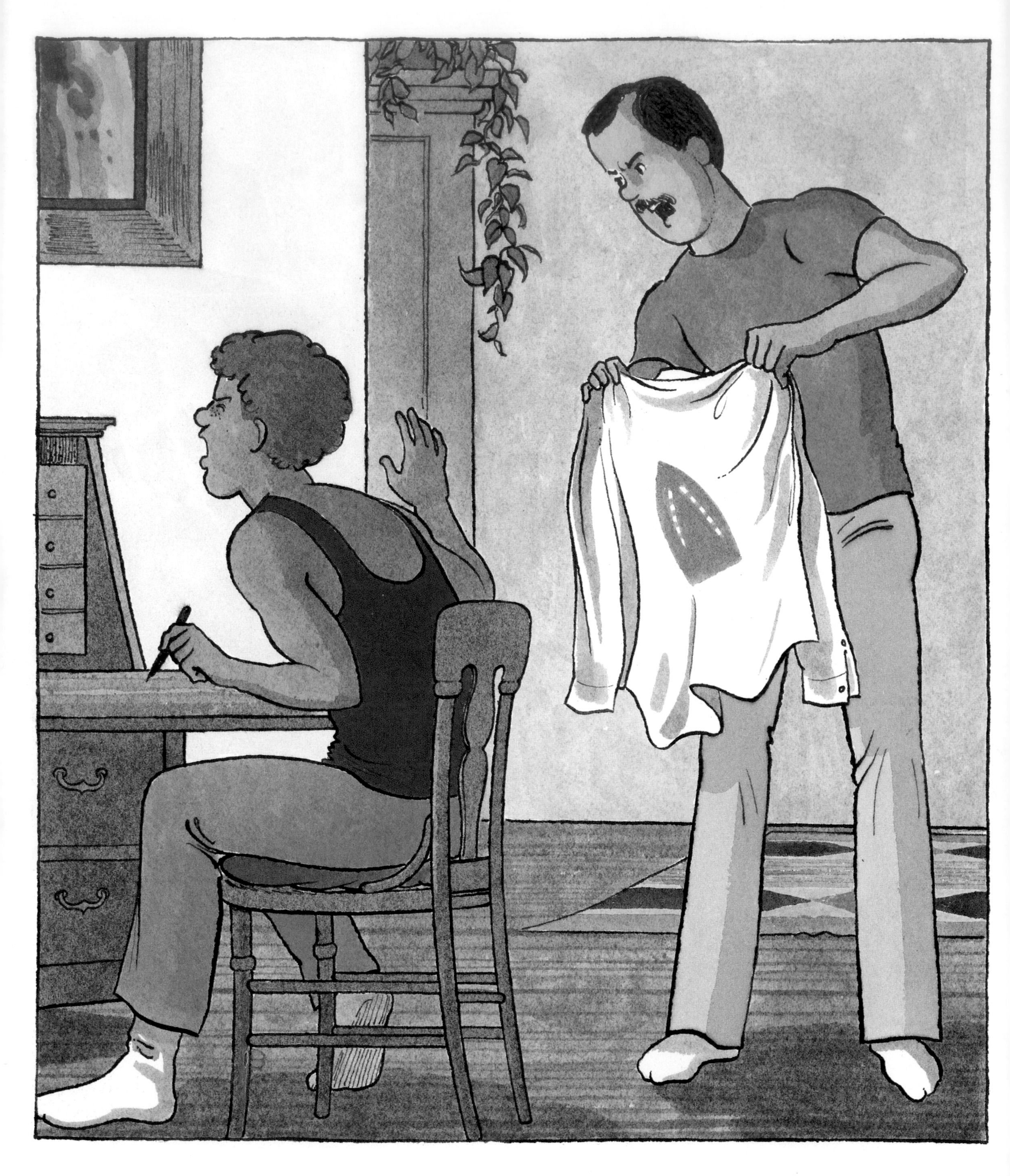

And sometimes even fight together,

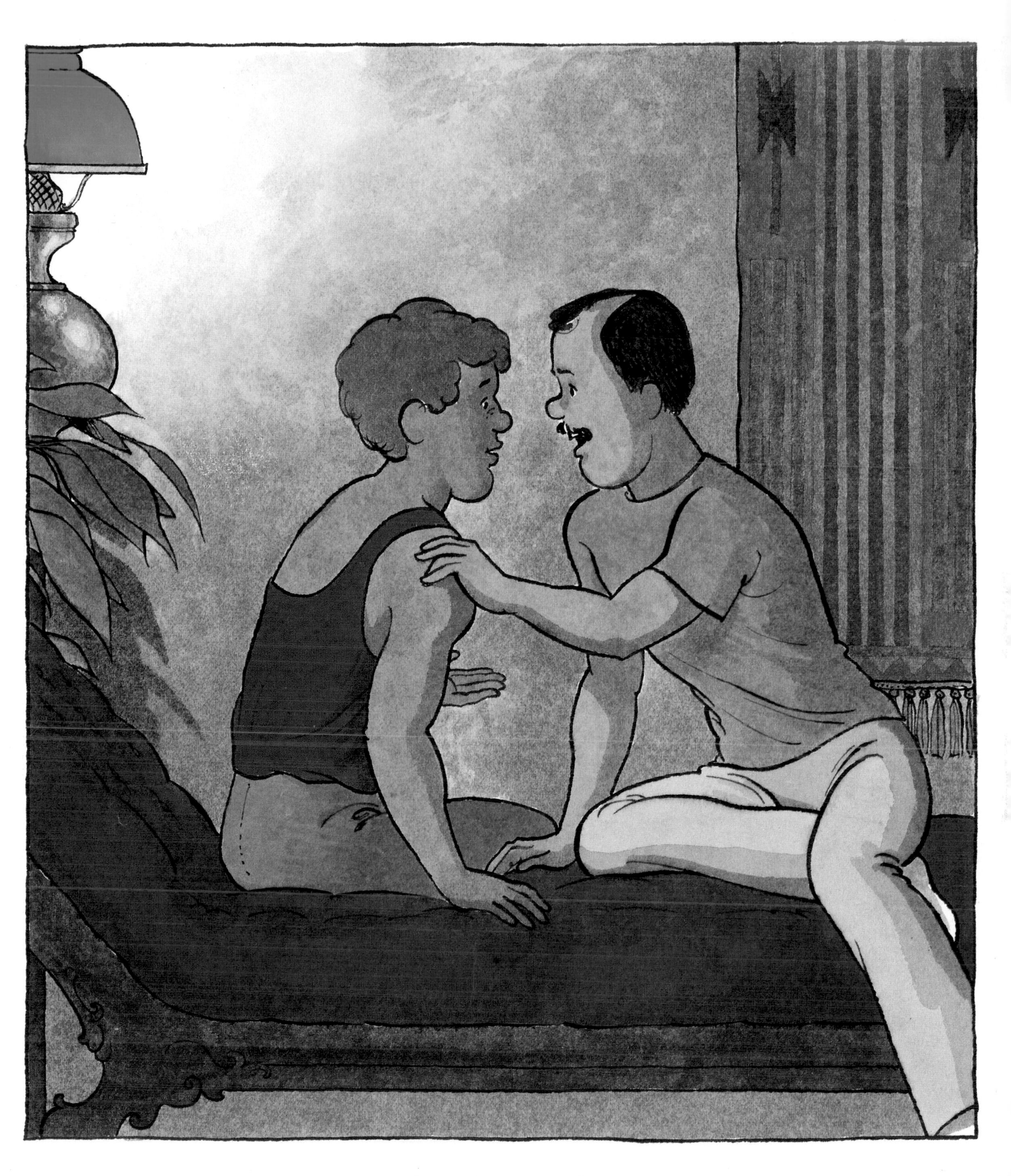

But they always make up.

Frank likes me too!

Just like Daddy, he tells me jokes and riddles,

Helps me catch bugs for show-and-tell,

Reads to me,

Makes *great* peanut butter-and-jelly sandwiches,

And chases nightmares away.

When weekends come,

we do all sorts of things together.

We go to ball games,

Visit the zoo,

Go to the beach,

Work in the yard,

Go shopping,

And in the evenings, we sing at the piano.

Mommy says Daddy and Frank are gay.

At first I didn’t know what that meant. So she explained it.

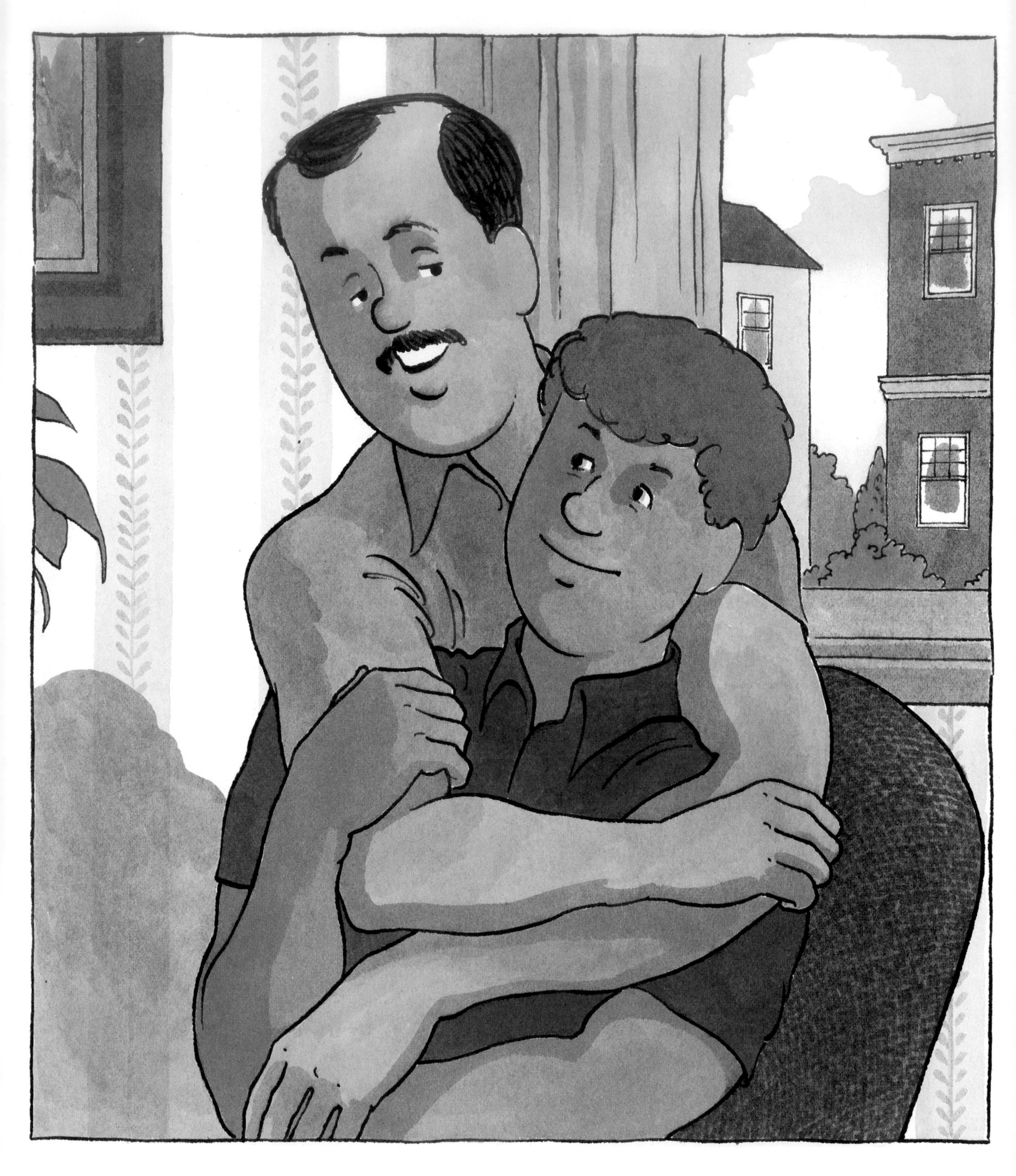

Being gay is just one more kind of love.

And love is the best kind of happiness.

Daddy and his roommate are very happy together,

And I'm happy too!